W0418709

Philip Hewitt

Tiger by the Tail

Ernst Klett Verlag
Stuttgart Düsseldorf Leipzig

Dieses Werk folgt im Deutschen der reformierten Rechtschreibung.

9 783125 482609

1. Auflage 1 9 8 7 6 | 2006 2005

Alle Drucke dieser Auflage können im Unterricht nebeeinander benutzt werden. Die letzte Zahl bezeichnet das Jahr dieses Druckes.

Umschlag: Duncan Smith, London.
Karte: Elsie Lennox, London.
Druck: Wilhelm Röck, Weinsberg.
Printed in Germany.

ISBN 3-12-548260-7

Contents

Chapter 1

It wasn't my idea to keep the money. I wanted to take it to the police as soon as we found it. It was all Alan's idea. We – that's my brother Alan and me (my name's Heather, by the way, and we're students) – we come from New Zealand and we were on a hitch-hiking trip around the world at the time. It sounds wonderful, doesn't it? And it was – for the first couple of months.

We travelled from New Zealand to Australia, where we had relations in Perth on the west coast. From there we went by boat to India, across India and over the Indian Ocean to East Africa. We saw Kenya, Tanzania and one or two other countries I can't remember much about. Then we got a cheap flight to Morocco and a ferry from North Africa to the south of Italy. Hitch-hiking in Europe wasn't as easy as we had thought, and we used up a lot of our money on buses and trains. When we finally got to Britain at the end of August, we were tired of travelling and staying in youth hostels. We were also running out of money. We only wanted to go home. The rest of the world could wait until next year.

After three days in London we decided to visit our Uncle Jeffrey in Oxford before flying back to New Zealand. We found his name in the Oxford phone book and rang the number. Luckily he was at home. He was very pleased to know that we were in Britain and invited us to come and stay with him for the weekend. We were on our way there when it all started.

Chapter 2

Alan saw the girl first. From the moment she sat down at a table two seats behind me until the moment the train left the station, I could tell that Alan was not listening to a word I was saying. He was looking at *her*. When the train began to move, I turned round and looked at her for a few seconds. She really was very attractive.

"Pretty girl," I said to him. "But not your type."

"Eh? Who?"

"That girl sitting behind me. Don't pretend! You can't take your eyes off her!"

"Don't be silly, Heather. She can't take her eyes off *me*! Look out! She's coming over!"

"Excuse me," said the girl with a smile, "but I saw the New Zealand flags on your rucksacks. I'm from Australia. Do you mind if I sit at your table and talk? I need help."

That was a dramatic start, anyway.

"Help? What kind of help?" I asked.

"First question: Are you going to Oxford?"

"Yes."

"OK, that's great. My name's Cathy, and I'm a secretary with a big Australian company in London. My boss had to go to a meeting in Oxford this morning, but he forgot some important documents and papers. He asked me to take the afternoon train to Oxford and meet him at the station with this briefcase."

"So what's the problem?" Alan asked.

"Well, it's Friday afternoon, and I live in Reading – that's the train's first stop in about twenty minutes. I'm meeting some friends at five o'clock. We want to go to a pop concert in Newbury tonight, and I've already paid for my ticket. My friends promised me a lift to Newbury, but they won't wait for me if I'm late, and I'll miss the concert anyway if I have to go all the way to Oxford and back. You could really help me if you wouldn't mind giving him this briefcase when you get to Oxford." She picked up a small black case off the seat beside her.

"Well ... I don't know ... ," Alan began. I suppose he thought there might be a bomb or something in it. We had seen the signs at the stations and heard the messages on the Underground: 'Keep your luggage with you at all times.' But it looked just like the normal kind of briefcase that every businessman carries. I picked it up. It was not heavy, so there were probably only papers in it. And Cathy didn't look like a terrorist to me, although I suppose there are beautiful terrorists, too!!

"I don't expect you to do it for nothing," Cathy went on. "Here's £20 for each of you. I'd really appreciate it ..." She smiled her sweetest smile. Alan could never resist a smile.

"OK, sport!" he said, in his best Australian accent. "It's a deal!"

Chapter 3

Cathy left the train at Reading a few minutes later, after she had given us a description of her boss, Mr John Rigby, and after thanking us once again for our help. Alan watched her walk towards the exit. She turned and waved. Alan waved back, but suddenly he stopped smiling.

"What is it, Alan?" I asked. The exit was behind me, so I couldn't see what was going on.

"Two policemen have just stopped Cathy ... They're talking to her now ..." Just as the train began to move, Alan jumped up. "Hey! I think they're arresting her!"

"That's impossible!" I said. "What for?"

"How should I know! It could be something to do with this briefcase. "

We both looked at the small black briefcase on the table between us. "Do you really think there can be any connection between the documents in the case and the police?" I asked him. "Maybe they're stolen. Do you think we should tell the police? Or should we just give them to Mr ... what was his name?"

"Rigby, John Rigby. Tall, brown hair, dark-grey business suit, copy of *The Times* newspaper under his left arm ..." that was more or less the description which Cathy had given us – all except the copy of *The Times*. That was something which Alan must have got from one of the old spy stories he was always reading.

"Do be serious for a minute, Alan! What should we *do*?"

"I can't think when I'm hungry! Isn't there a buffet car on this train?"

"Right behind you. I saw it when we got on."

"Coffee and a sandwich? We can afford it now!" and he walked off with Cathy's £20 note in his hand.

Two minutes later he was back, but without the food and drink. And he looked very pale.

"What's the matter now?" I asked.

"That £20 note," he said, taking it out of his pocket and tearing it into two halves. "The £20 note she gave us was a forgery. A good one, but still a forgery!"

Chapter 4

I looked at the two halves of the £20 note on the table in front of me and sighed: "That's just bad luck. Don't you remember? The bank told us about all these forgeries before we left New Zealand. England is full of them. They told us to be careful. Maybe Cathy wasn't careful enough. How did the buffet car attendant know it was a forgery?"

"They've got these ultra-violet testers everywhere now," he said. "Even on trains. They check all the big banknotes. Let's see yours."

I took it out of my purse and gave it to him. "Look, Heather: the numbers are consecutive. Mine's N 71 591585, yours is N 71 591586. They're both forgeries. Now I think I know why the police were waiting for our friend Cathy at Reading Station. They were expecting to find this," he said, pointing to the small black briefcase. "She wants us to hand it over to her boss at Oxford. Maybe he doesn't know that the police are watching her. She's in the clear because she's passed the loot on to us! Very clever!"

"Loot?"

"Well, no prizes for guessing what's in the briefcase, Heather! Not important business papers. I should think it's full of forged £20 notes, just like the ones Cathy gave us. You realize what she's done, don't you? She's made us her accomplices!"

"But surely we can just take the briefcase to the police in Oxford and tell them what happened," I argued.

"Do you think they'd believe us? Two penniless New Zealanders who've just tried to pass a forged £20 note in a railway buffet car? I'll be surprised if they don't arrest us at Oxford Station when we arrive – the buffet car attendant has probably already phoned the police. If they catch us with that briefcase full of forged banknotes, we're going to have a lot of explaining to do. If Cathy's boss sees the cops at the station, he'll probably guess what's happened. He'll just walk away leaving us with the dud notes. No, the best thing to do is to leave the case on the seat and get off at the next station. What's the next station?"

"Oxford," I said unhappily.

Alan looked even unhappier. "Well, we'll stay on the train – hide in the toilet – and get off at the next station after Oxford. Come on!"

There was just about room for the two of us, our back-packs and the black briefcase in the toilet. I looked at Alan and he looked at me.

"Before the police arrest us, Heather," he said, "I'd like to see what I'm going to prison for!"

The briefcase was locked, of course, but Alan took his big knife out of his rucksack and slid it between the two halves of the briefcase. He turned the knife, and the locks opened with a loud double snap.

A shower of banknotes rained down onto the toilet floor. Fives, tens, twenties and fifties. And these notes were old and looked genuine enough.

"Holy smoke!" was all that Alan could say.

At that moment the train began to slow down, and a voice over the loudspeaker announced: "In a few minutes this train will be arriving at Oxford Station. Oxford next stop!"

Chapter 5

By the time we had picked up all the banknotes and put them back into the briefcase, the train was already leaving Oxford, so we never saw what – if anything – was happening on the platform. Whether Mr Rigby was really waiting there in his dark-grey business suit with or without a copy of *The Times* under his left arm, or whether the buffet car attendant got off to 'have a quiet word' with a couple of policemen or not. To be honest, I was too worried to care.

Only seconds after the train had begun to move there was a loud knock at the door. Terrified, I stared at Alan. "What is it?" he shouted angrily.

"Tickets from Oxford, please!" was the simple answer. It was the ticket inspector.

"We got on at Paddington, mate!" Alan shouted back.

"*We*? How many of you in there?"

"Just me – my sister has got our tickets. She's in the buffet car."

The ticket inspector walked away. Alan opened the door. "He's gone! Come on!"

"Come on? Where to?"

"To the front of the train. He's going towards the back. We haven't got tickets to the next station. What is the next station, anyway?"

"How on earth should I know!"

"OK, OK! No need to get angry!" And he walked off down the corridor.

Miserably, I followed. We found seats in a fairly empty part of the train and sat down.

"What are we going to do now?" was all I could think of saying. "We're on our way to the next station down the line – whatever the place is called. We have a briefcase full of money that belongs to the mysterious Mr Rigby, whose secretary or assistant has just been arrested. Uncle Jeffrey will be wondering why we haven't arrived at Oxford ..."

"Just let me think for a few minutes, Heather," said Alan.

So I sat back and watched the green English countryside rolling past the train window while Alan thought.

He was still thinking when the train began to slow down and the voice on the loudspeaker announced Banbury as the next station.

"No good ideas yet?" I asked Alan as we picked up our packs and the black briefcase, and walked to the door.

"Not yet, Heather. Give me time," was all he said.

We got off the train at Banbury, found a telephone and tried to ring Uncle Jeffrey, but there was no one at home. He had probably gone to the station to meet our train.

It was six o'clock now, and there was nothing left to do but walk off into town in search of a B & B place to spend the night.

We found one in Oxford Road. It was a big house run by a friendly old lady called Mrs Parr. She told us to make ourselves at home while she got our room ready and prepared our supper, so we sat down in the TV lounge to watch the news. It was towards the end of the news that we both sat up and listened.

"Today the police came a step nearer to solving the mystery of the flood of forged £20 notes in the south of England," the newsreader was saying. "This evening a young woman was helping Thames Valley Police with their inquiries. The young woman, who has not been named ..."

"That must be Cathy!"

"Ssh!" hissed Alan.

"... but who works at the London branch of the Bank of Australia, may be involved in putting forged £20 notes into circulation during normal banking business. And now the weather ..."

"Now we know where all that money comes from," said Alan. "Cathy must have exchanged the genuine notes at the bank where she works for forged £20 ones and was on her way to Oxford to give the money to Rigby. They must be accomplices."

"It certainly looks that way," I said, "Poor Cathy! She never got to her pop concert after all! But what are we going to do with the money, Alan? We can't just keep it."

"Well, it's too late to do anything about it today," he said. "I'm tired. Supper's nearly ready. Let's just sleep on it."

And that's exactly what we did.

Chapter 6

The next day was Saturday, and we slept a little longer than we had planned. Mrs Parr knocked gently on our door with the news: "Breakfast's ready – it's nearly nine o'clock!"

We ate our cornflakes in silence and listened to the nine o'clock news as we ate. Again Cathy's story was one of the last items: "The Australian woman questioned by police yesterday in connection with the flood of forged £20 notes was released late last night as there was no evidence to link her to the crime ..."

"That's because *we've* got the evidence," whispered Alan, as Mrs Parr brought in our bacon and eggs. It was difficult to enjoy the traditional English breakfast knowing that we were wandering around the country with £100,000 – we had counted it the night before – of someone else's money in our backpacks.

"So what's your plan, Master Mind?" I whispered back.

"I'm still thinking," was all he said. Then, after he had thought for a minute, he suddenly said. "We'll need some more cash. Have you still got any traveller's cheques?"

"I think I have a couple left. But aren't British banks closed all day on Saturdays?" They weren't. Mrs Parr told us that Barclays Bank in the High Street would be open until twelve o'clock.

We left our backpacks in the room and wandered into town. It was not far to the High Street, where we soon found the Banbury branch of Barclays Bank.

There were not many people in the bank that Saturday morning. A video camera moved slowly to and fro, watching every move we made. I stuck out my tongue at it and immediately wished I hadn't.

"Can I help you?" asked an intelligent-looking young clerk who would probably be able to give the police a perfect description of the two of us.

"I'd like to change a traveller's cheque for $200," I said. He took my cheque and began to fill in a form. "May I see your passport, please?"

I passed it to him, and he carefully wrote down my full name, passport number and perhaps even my height, colour of eyes, birthday: everything that would identify me to the police! Then he asked for our address in Banbury. "We're only here for the weekend," I explained. "We're going back to London tomorrow."

He looked at us slightly suspiciously. "It's just a formality, but I must have the address where you spent last night – please." The 'please' sounded a bit like a formality, too.

"Mrs Parr's Guest House, 83 Oxford Road, Banbury," said Alan. The clerk noted it down as if he didn't quite believe him.

"Just a moment, please," he said. He walked to the back of the bank, where he began talking to an older woman. The woman looked at us and nodded to him. Then she walked into an office at the back of the bank – to phone the police? – while the young clerk came back to the counter.

"How would you like your cash?"

"I beg your pardon?" I asked, wondering if I should say: 'As quickly as possible'.

"£126 in fives, tens or twenties?"

It was Alan who answered in a voice loud enough for everybody in the bank to hear: "We'd better have it in tenners, please. They say there are a lot of dud twenties about nowadays."

There was a frosty silence as we left the bank. Everyone was watching us. As we walked out I almost expected to be met by two policemen, or to hear the alarm bell ring, but nothing happened.

"Now what?" I asked Alan, stopping suddenly.

"Let's do a bit of sightseeing. This is the first small town in Britain that we've visited. It's a pity about Oxford, but perhaps we can stop there on our way back to London – unless you're afraid of the mysterious Mr. Rigby."

"Perhaps we'd better give it a miss," I said. "But we should try and ring Uncle Jeffrey again."

"We can do that later. I want to take some photos while the sun's shining."

We walked around the market, which sold almost everything from food to clothing. Alan bought some postcards and a silly T-shirt which said 'Keep Britain Tidy' on the front and 'Drop your litter in France' on the back.

After a while we left the market and walked up the High Street, looking in the shop windows. It was while we were looking at the clothes in the window of one of the clothes shops that I noticed the car. It was a big black car, and the only reason I noticed it was because it looked so out of place in a small English town, and because it was moving at the same speed as we were walking. We walked about fifty yards up the street and stopped again. Sure enough, the big black car stopped right opposite the shop.

"Don't look now," I said to Alan, "but I think we're being followed."

"I know," he said quietly. "But I didn't think you'd noticed. He's been following us since we left the bank, in fact. But I think I know how to lose him. Come on."

The next shop was Woolworths, and we walked straight in the front entrance and out of the emergency exit at the back. As soon as Alan touched the door, an alarm began to ring. One of the assistants shouted "Stop!" – it sounded very much like "Stop thief!" but the last thing we were going to do was stop. We ran out of the door and found ourselves in a small courtyard. Luckily there was a way out into a back-street.

"Taxi!" shouted Alan, and as if by magic a taxi suddenly stopped right in front of us. We jumped in. "Where to?" asked the driver. "83 Oxford Road," I said. As the driver turned into the High Street, I put my hand up to hide my face and looked between two fingers at the side of the street opposite Woolworths. The big black car was still parked outside. In the driving seat was a man who looked as if he might have been the world heavyweight boxing champion in about 1980.

Cathy was sitting in the seat beside him. She was looking straight ahead – I only saw her face for a second and it was hard to tell whether she was very angry or very frightened.

Suddenly I wished we had never met her.

Chapter 7

We spent the afternoon in our room, wondering how Cathy had found out where we were.

"She probably put two and two together," Alan suggested, "and when we didn't hand the briefcase over to Mr Rigby at Oxford Station, she – or they – probably decided to check out the towns on the train's route. They were lucky. We got off at the first stop after Oxford and they found us straight away. They may even have been waiting outside the bank."

"I still think we should go to the police and tell them what's happened."

Obviously Alan disagreed with me, for he said nothing. I was beginning to worry that he might have ideas of keeping the money. Why else would he refuse to give it up? Then, late in the afternoon, he told me. I had never thought of my brother as an idealist, or a crusader against organized crime, but that was exactly what he turned out to be. All the time he had been thinking out his plan. Now he explained it to me.

"If Rigby & Co. can chase us round Britain like this, they're obviously criminals. They must belong to a fairly big organization. Crime is big business today, Heather, just as big business is sometimes very close to crime. I don't know how Cathy got involved in all this, but she made a big mistake when she gave us that briefcase, and she's paying for it now. The big guy driving that black car didn't look like anybody's favourite uncle. I hate to think what would happen to her – or us – if we just handed the money in at the police station. The people it belongs to could get very angry. They might leave us alone, but what about Cathy?"

"So you think we should hand it back to Rigby & Co.?"

"That might be easier, but even if we handed the brief-case back, we would still know what was inside it, remember? It's all my fault for opening it! We're in quite a mess, aren't we? These people are crooks. Maybe Cathy is an accomplice – maybe she isn't. But I have the feeling that this is a big gang of well-organized criminals."

"The Mafia?"

"Maybe, maybe not. But anyone who can flood the country with forged banknotes must be into crime in a serious way. If we hand the money in to the police, the people who are chasing us will take their revenge. They can get pretty nasty with people who double-cross them. What I'd like to do is get the police interested in *us*."

"Get *ourselves* arrested?" I was horrified. "That's what I thought we've been trying to avoid for the last two days!"

"No, Heather, that's not what I mean. If Rigby & Co. are on our trail, the best thing would be to get the police to chase *us*. In that way they'd be chasing the gang at the same time. If we're lucky, the police will be on the spot when the gang catches up with us. The police will see that we're not accomplices."

"And if we're *un*lucky?"

"We mustn't even think about that. We'll have to take our chances. If we give the money to the police the gang will be angrier than if they catch us with it. We've got a tiger by the tail."

"Tiger by the tail?"

"It's an old Indian saying, Heather, but it's still very true today. What should you never do if you're holding onto a tiger's tail?"

"I don't know."

"You should never let go! You have to hold on."

"So we go back to London tomorrow?"

"No. That's what Rigby & Co. will expect us to do. We've got to disappear for a few days – until the police start to follow our, and their, trail. We'll organize some kind of paper chase."

"Paper chase?"

"Yes. Uncle Jeffrey will begin to worry about us soon. He might even tell the police. We'll leave a trail of clues for the police to follow. Rigby & Co. managed to find us. Let's see if the police can do the same!"

"And what if nobody 'misses' us?" I asked.

"Well, we'll just have to think of something else."

"Like what?"

"I don't know, Heather. But I've done enough thinking for one day."

Alan picked up a book and started to read. I did the same.

"What are you reading?" I asked.

"An early Le Carré story: *The Spy Who Came in from the Cold*."

It seemed a very suitable title for our adventure. I was shivering already.

Chapter 8

We did not sleep well that night, and not even the full English breakfast on Sunday morning could cheer us up. We packed our things, said goodbye to Mrs Parr and made sure that she knew we were going to Birmingham next. We had dropped our first clue in Alan's paper chase. We looked carefully up and down the street before leaving the house, and although there was no sign of the big black car, I couldn't help feeling that it was not far away. It wouldn't take them long to ask about two New Zealanders at all the hotels and guest houses in Banbury. They would soon be on our track if Mrs Parr told them we were heading for Birmingham.

The briefcase with the money was safely hidden in Alan's backpack.

As it was Sunday, there was not much traffic on the road. But we were lucky. We had only been waiting for ten minutes when a lorry stopped.

"Where you going?" the driver asked.

"Birmingham," I said.

"OK. I can take you there. Get in." And we did.

Luckily there was plenty of room in the cab for three people and two backpacks. The driver was a young man – not much older than us – and he told us that he was on his way to Glasgow.

"Glasgow?" said Alan. "How far away is that?"

"Och, five hundred miles or so. Will ye no' change your minds?"

"I beg your pardon?"

"Sorry – my Scots accent ... Won't you change your minds? Birmingham's no place for tourists. You could be in Bonnie Scotland in time for dinner this evening. There's a fine youth hostel in Glasgow, and from there you can go north to the Highlands. The scenery in the Highlands is grand! By the way, my name's Andrew – but you can call me Andy."

The countryside we were passing through was a scenery of rolling, green hills, and it reminded me a bit of New Zealand, only there were more cattle than sheep in this part of North Oxfordshire. After about an hour we were driving through Birmingham on the M6 motorway. We didn't see much of the city centre, but we both agreed that we would rather stay in the lorry as far as Glasgow. Andy smiled.

It was early afternoon now, and the sun was shining brightly. When we had left Birmingham and the other industrial towns of the Midlands behind us, we both began to enjoy the ride. Mr Rigby and his gang seemed a long way away.

As we drove north up the M6 the hills began to get higher. "Those are the Pennines on your right," said Andy, pointing to a line of hills in the distance, "and the Lake District away on your left."

As we drove north past the Lake District, the countryside became wilder. We were driving through a land of rolling hills and moorland. There were more sheep than cattle in the fields, which were surrounded by stone walls.

Finally we crossed the border into Scotland, and when we crossed a small river, Andy gave a happy shout: "Look! That's the Clyde, Glasgow's river. It doesn't look very big here, but wait until you see it at Glasgow!"

At last we reached Glasgow. Andy dropped us at the corner of George Square in the centre of town and said he would come back and pick us up in his car in about an hour when he had taken the truck back to the depot. He wanted to show us the town and drive us to a youth hostel near the city centre.

"Let's get a Sunday paper to read while we're waiting," I suggested as we were passing a newspaper shop which was still open even on a Sunday evening.

We sat down on a seat near the corner where Andy had said he would meet us. Alan had bought two papers: the *Sunday Times* and the *Sunday Mirror,* probably because he wanted to be sure not to miss any sensational news items.

"I'll read the *Sunday Times*, you read the *Sunday*

Mirror. Keep your eyes open for anything about Cathy."

I didn't have to keep my eyes open for long. Almost immediately I saw the news item we were looking for. The headline said: AUSTRALIAN EX-GLAMOUR GIRL VANISHES. Underneath was a photo of Cathy. I was just about to show Alan the article when he said: "Hey! Just listen to this, Heather!: BANK OF AUSTRALIA CLERK DISAPPEARS – there's a photo of Cathy and two policemen outside Reading Station. Listen to this ..."

"Ssh! – Idiot! Not so loud!" I hissed. Several people had turned round to stare at Alan. "Read it yourself first – there's something in my paper, too. We don't want people to know that we know her, do we?"

We both read our articles in silence before exchanging papers and reading the story all over again. My article was – like the newspaper – quite sensational. Here it is in full:

AUSTRALIAN EX-GLAMOUR GIRL VANISHES.

The bank clerk and ex-model from Sydney, Australia, who was arrested on Friday in connection with the flood of forged £20 notes in London and southern England, and who was released on Saturday morning, has disappeared. Sunday Mirror reporters who went to talk to her at her London flat yesterday afternoon were told that she had left in the company of a tall, well-built man within minutes of arriving home that morning. "We have no idea where Ms Wilson is," said a spokesman for Scotland Yard, "but as there is no evidence to link her with any crime, we do not suspect foul play."

"Poor Cathy!" whispered Alan. "It certainly looks as if she's been kidnapped! I was afraid this might happen. So nobody knows where she is, eh?" He thought for a moment, stood up and wandered off in the direction of a telephone box.

I went on reading the paper. There was an attractive advertisement for a new car on one of the middle pages: THE NEW ROVER 216i – DRIVE IT AWAY FOR ONLY £9,999. I suddenly realized that we were carrying enough money to buy ten of them!

Alan came back smiling.

"What are you looking so pleased about?" I asked.

"I've just dropped the next clue in our paper chase. I've rung the police to tell them that we saw Cathy yesterday in Banbury driving around in a big black car with someone who looked like the man mentioned in the newspaper article, Heather."

I was horrified. "Did you tell them who we were?"

"Of course not. I just said we were two New Zealanders on holiday in Scotland – that's a big enough hint to start them off – and before the policeman could ask me any more questions, my money ran out. You can't telephone long for 10p."

So that was that. The paper chase had begun. Now we really had the tiger by the tail!

Just then we heard a car horn and saw Andy waving to us from a bright red Mini. We got in – there was just about room for the backpacks – and Andy drove off on his promised tour of the city he loved so well.

When we had seen just about everything there was to see, he drove us to the youth hostel as promised. He asked us how long we would be staying in Glasgow, and when we said two nights, maybe three, he shook his head.

"One night is plenty, and you've seen almost all the sights already. You should move on tomorrow. Go further north and see something of the *real* Scotland: Loch Lomond is a grand place to start. It's not far north of Glasgow." He thought for a moment. "An aunt of mine lives in Crianlarich – it's a little place up in the hills north of Loch Lomond. Beautiful scenery! She does bed-and-breakfast during the summer. If you travel north by train you'll have to go through her village anyway. I'll give you her address and telephone number."

I noted them down. I never thought at the time that we might need them, but we did – and much sooner than we realized.

Chapter 9

The next morning we couldn't make up our minds whether to stay another night in Glasgow or to move on, but the girl at the reception desk said: "We've got two big groups of young people arriving today, so we'll be very full, and if you check out now, we can't promise you a bed if you come back in the afternoon. And if you want to spend tonight here, I shall have to ask you to pay for your accommodation in advance."

"What do you think, Heather?" Alan asked me.

"We'd better have one more night here, I think."

So we paid.

I had a sudden premonition and as we were about to walk out into the sunshine for a second look at the city, I said to Alan: "Let's not leave our backpacks here, Alan."

"Why not? They're too heavy to carry about all day. They'll be safer here than on our backs – and lighter, too!"

"It's a feeling I have, that's all."

"All right, Heather. We can put them in a locker at one of the stations if they get too heavy. And the loot will be safer if we carry it around with us."

Secretly I was still hoping that Alan would somehow give up his idea of using us as bait to catch the Mafia, or whoever was following us, but he still seemed to be enjoying his paper chase! The police would probably be looking for us now, too. We certainly had a tiger by the tail!

It was a warm morning, so we soon got tired of walking around with heavy packs on our backs. We had a cup of coffee in a café near the city centre and thought about our next move. Alan had bought a tourist map of Scotland and we were soon following the railway line to Fort William with our fingers. It ran past the top of Loch Lomond, the lake which Andy had said was so beautiful, and it certainly looked attractive, even on a map. There were all kinds of symbols showing tourist attractions all around the loch: youth hostels, fishing, sailing, canoeing, windsurfing ...

"I think we should move north tomorrow." said Alan. "We can either stay at one of the youth hostels on Loch Lomond or maybe even with Andy's aunt at that little village he mentioned – here it is: Crianlarich. It's on the main road north. It's on the railway line, too, so it shouldn't be hard to get there even if we can't hitch a lift. Then we'll have to make sure Rigby & Co. know where we are. It doesn't look as if they've managed to follow us all the way to Glasgow."

We looked out of the window for a minute or two, but there was no sign of the big black car which had nearly found us in Banbury two days before.

"You look as if you're actually *hoping* to see that car!" I said.

Alan smiled, but I could tell he was worried about the risks we were taking. "Well, when they get too close to us, Heather, we'll just have to make sure the police aren't too far away. We've got to get the police interested enough to follow us, too."

"Another phone call?"

"Not before we're ready to leave Glasgow. If we go north by train, which station would we leave from?"

"I've no idea ..."

But the girl behind the café counter knew, and it didn't take Alan long to find out that we would be leaving from Queen Street Station. It was in the centre of the city, not too far from the youth hostel.

"Let's go there now and find out about train times. The girl says there aren't more than five trains a day. I don't think I'd like to have to stand around waiting for long at a station. There are always policemen about."

So we paid for our coffee, picked up our packs and walked to Queen Street Station.

"Look!" I cried. "Luggage lockers! Let's leave our packs here. Then we can pick them up on our way back to the hostel this evening."

Before we put our heavy packs in two of the biggest lockers, Alan decided it would be better to put the brief-case in my pack. "You've got more room, and it's your turn to carry it, anyway," he said. I didn't think at the time that he might have another reason for switching packs, but as it turned out he did. We locked the doors and put the keys in our pockets. Then we walked across to the information office and picked up two leaflets giving the times of trains to the Highlands and showing some of the fine scenery we could expect to see on our journey north. By then the alarm-clock in Alan's stomach was telling him that it was nearly lunch time. We felt a bit hot and sticky after our morning's walk, so we wandered back towards the youth hostel to have a wash first.

It was Alan who saw the police car stop outside the youth hostel. Luckily we were not carrying our luggage, so we didn't look like two young foreign tourists. Two policemen got out of the car and walked in.

We watched them from the other side of the street. The girl at the desk was obviously checking the list of guests, and we could imagine the question-and-answer routine that was going on inside: "Young New Zealanders? Yes, Sergeant, we've got two who arrived yesterday and are staying here tonight. Names? Just a second ... Can I describe them? Well, the young man is about six feet tall, dark hair, brown eyes, sun-tanned. His sister? Long blond hair, blue eyes, quite attractive, about five feet ten. They didn't say when they were coming back ..."

Well, we knew the answer to that. Never.

One of the policemen sat down in a comfortable armchair and began to read a newspaper.

"Good," said Alan. "They're on our track at last! It was a good idea not to leave our packs there. Well done, Heather!"

I was not so happy. "That means we can't stay in Glasgow – and we can't stay at any other youth hostel. The police will soon find us there. Where do we go from here, Master Mind?"

Alan thought for a moment. "We'd better stay at a B & B place. Perhaps Andy's aunt will have a room free."

"We could phone her," I suggested.

"No. Let's leave our options open. When's the next train north, Heather?"

I looked at our timetable. "Not until 16.40. Then there's one at 20.40, but it doesn't get to Crianlarich until 22.22. That's a bit late if we want to find accommodation, isn't it?"

"You're right. 16.40 it is, then. We'll walk around until about four. But let's have some lunch first."

At last it was time to take a bus to the station. We bought our tickets ten minutes before the train was due to leave. Then we walked to the lockers to pick up our backpacks.

Then disaster.

Alan couldn't find his locker key! He looked through all his pockets and I even looked in all of mine, but we could not find the key, and precious minutes were ticking away. Finally, he gave up.

"I must have dropped it somewhere. Damn and blast it! I'm sorry, Heather. You'll have to go ahead without me."

"Without you ...?"

"You'll be OK! Someone has to arrange our accommodation. I'll catch the later train and you can meet me at Crianlarich station. I'll tell the people at the left-luggage office that I've lost my key and they'll open the locker for me. I can identify my backpack all right. It's lucky we put the money in your pack!"

But I was beginning to panic. "Can't you get them to open the locker *now*, Alan. Or let me wait ... Don't let's split up! If anything happens to you ..."

"Nothing will happen to me, Heather. I'll be all right. I'll see you at 22.22 tonight in Crianlarich. You'll have to run – your train's nearly due to leave! Give me my ticket and a couple of pounds." I gave him the ticket and a ten-pound note from my purse, and ran.

I just managed to board the train before the automatic doors shut.

Chapter 10

I don't remember much about the first part of the journey. I was too worried about Alan and had hated to leave him and go on alone. And I was carrying the money. Suppose Rigby & Co. caught me before Alan arrived? What on earth would I do?

As I had no answers to these questions, I finally decided to try and enjoy the trip. The railway ran along the Clyde for a while, then up the side of Gare Loch and Loch Long until it reached the northern end of Loch Lomond at a place called Ardlui. The scenery got more beautiful the further away we got from Glasgow. The hills were real mountains now, and getting higher all the time.

The next station after Ardlui was Crianlarich, and the first person I saw when I stepped onto the platform was Cathy.

Luckily she didn't see me, because I was just one of many backpackers who got off the train here. But there was no mistaking the beautiful Cathy. She was looking the other way, so I dodged behind one of the station buildings and waited for the train to leave. It seemed in no hurry to go, and I suddenly guessed why. The line north and the line from Glasgow up which I had come was single track. Crianlarich was where trains from south and north crossed. My train was waiting for the train from Fort William to Glasgow to arrive, and this train was obviously late.

How on earth did Cathy know I would be arriving on this train? Had they caught Alan already? Had he told them where I – and the money – would be?

Then I realized that Cathy might be waiting for someone on the train from Fort William. No wonder she had been looking the other way. She hadn't been waiting for my train at all! Perhaps she did not even know that I was on the same platform!

One thing really shocked me, though. Rigby & Co. seemed to be even quicker than the police! They had followed us all the way to Scotland, and Cathy had actually arrived at Crianlarich *before* me! What chance did we have of keeping one step ahead of them for much longer?

Then I heard the sound of a locomotive horn in the distance. It echoed from one hillside to the other and back again, although the train was still a couple of miles away. It was signalling its late arrival to the driver of the Fort William train. Whoever Cathy was waiting for would soon be arriving. Cathy had not been kidnapped. She must be one of the gang!

After what seemed an age I finally heard, in the distance, the sound of the approaching train. At last the locomotive came in sight and slowly the train slid to a stop in the station. People began to get off. I was terrified that Cathy might look round suddenly or come walking along the platform towards me. But she stayed exactly where she was, and very soon she was joined by a tall, thin man with brown hair wearing a dark grey business suit, and although he was not carrying a copy of *The Times* under his arm, I recognized him from Cathy's description.

It was Mr Rigby himself.

Chapter 11

Cathy and Rigby stood on the platform talking for some minutes. I was not close enough to hear what they were saying, but I felt they knew they were getting closer to their £100,000 every minute. I hoped they didn't realize at that very moment that they could almost have reached out and touched it!

Luckily the station exit was behind them, so when they turned and walked down the steps into the tunnel under the tracks, I was able to follow them at a safe distance. Outside, in the station car park, was the big black car. The boxing champion was sitting at the wheel. Cathy and Rigby got in, and the car drove off down the road. It turned north away from the village, and I felt a bit safer then.

It was now almost seven o'clock – high time to phone Mrs Macpherson, Andy's aunt, and ask her if she could give us B & B for the night. There was a telephone box outside the station, so I went in and dialled her number.

Mrs Macpherson said she had a room free and explained how to get to her house. It was in the main street. Number 68. Crianlarich is a small place, and within ten minutes I was standing outside the door of a small terraced house. I looked for the piece of paper with the address on it to check the house number, but I must have left it in the phone box! Another contribution to Alan's paper chase! But suppose Cathy or Rigby came back and found it – and me? Oh well, I thought. Too late to worry about that now.

I rang the bell. The door opened and a small woman of about fifty smiled at me: "Come in, dear, and make yourself at home. Where's your brother?"

"Alan will be arriving on the later train," I explained. "He sent me on ahead to find accommodation for the night."

"Well, come in. You look quite tired. Take off that big rucksack and sit down in the living-room. You're just in time for the news on TV. My husband won't be back until later. Can you wait an hour for your dinner, or would you like a sandwich now?"

I felt quite hungry, but said I would wait. Mrs Macpherson sat down to watch the seven o'clock news with me. The international news was the normal mixture of mini wars, trouble in Northern Ireland and ecological problems. This was worrying enough, but I was waiting to see if there had been any developments in our own story. Were the police still looking for Cathy? Had the hunt for the forgers moved to Scotland? But there was nothing on the news. Had the police given up already?

The next programme on TV was a soap opera I had never seen before. You know the kind of thing: it's no good watching one part unless you've seen most of the others, so I asked if I could have a shower before supper. Mrs Macpherson told me to take my time. Dinner would be ready when her husband got home at about eight.

There would still be two hours to kill before I could meet Alan at the station. I put on my best clothes and was just coming downstairs when I heard a key in the front door. It would be Mr Macpherson, home from a long day at the office or wherever he worked and ready for his dinner. I put on my friendliest smile, but the smile died on my lips. It was not Mr Macpherson but *Sergeant* Macpherson who was waiting for me at the bottom of the stairs. He was not smiling, and Cathy was with him.

Chapter 12

"A fine mess you and your brother have got yourselves into!" was the first thing Sergeant Macpherson said. I didn't try to protest. He obviously knew who I was. I expected him to arrest me on the spot, but he just hung up his jacket and kissed his wife on the cheek.

Mrs Macpherson seemed surprised to see another guest arriving at such a late hour, but just nodded when her husband told her that there would be yet another visitor after dinner: Inspector March of Scotland Yard.

"Yes," said Cathy, looking at me. "Don't look so shocked, Heather! I'm on your side after all. Alan is safe, and he'll be free as soon as we hand the money over."

"You mean Alan's a prisoner? Where?"

"I think I'd better explain," began Cathy. "But I can't do it here in the hall."

"You two go into the front room," said the sergeant. "I'll leave Ms Wilson to explain the situation to you. This isn't official police business yet – not until the inspector from Scotland Yard gets here, at least."

So we went into the front room and sat down. Cathy began her story.

"The first thing is not to worry about Alan. He's safe and I know exactly where he is. I'm sure you both thought that I was a member of the gang of forgers, but that's what I wanted everybody to believe. I've been on your side all the time! I work at the Bank of Australia, like it says in the papers, but I'm not just a clerk. I work in the Security Branch – a kind of private bank police. Rigby is the boss of an Australian gang of forgers who have been bringing forged British banknotes, printed in Hong Kong, into the country. My job was to join the gang and promise to help them to replace genuine Bank of England notes at my bank with their excellent forgeries. No one would suspect £20 notes fresh from the bank. I told Rigby that my job was to check all notes coming into the bank, and said that I would 'pass' a certain number of forged notes every day. That was about a month ago. Other people have been passing the forged notes for much longer. That's why there are so many forgeries in circulation at the moment. Of course I didn't actually pass any of the forgeries on, but I knew that at the end of a month I would have to give Rigby the same amount in genuine notes."

"The money in the briefcase?"

"That's right. We put an electronic homing device in the briefcase so that we would be able to follow the money wherever it went. That's how we knew where to find you. The plan was to arrest Rigby and the rest of the gang after he had got the briefcase. But I made one mistake which ruined my plan: I must have given you two of Rigby's counterfeit notes by mistake! The forgeries are so perfect that only an ultra-violet tester can distinguish them from the genuine article."

"But why didn't you give him the briefcase yourself?" I asked.

"The three important members of the gang were in different parts of the country at the time. The second part of my plan was to appear to be arrested by the police and force Rigby to panic. If he thought the police were getting close to him, he would probably call a meeting of the big members of the gang. He would take the briefcase with him, and we would follow him. The police would then be able to catch not just Rigby but his accomplices, too."

"Well, your plan nearly worked. We heard about your 'arrest' on the TV, and Rigby must have been very worried when you didn't turn up at Oxford Station!"

"He was! But he was even more worried when you didn't keep your promise to hand the money over to him. Now we had to start all over again. When the police 'released' me the next day, I contacted Rigby and explained what had happened. I said I had given the money to you because the police were already on my tail. I told him I knew you were staying in Banbury, and I was in the car with Rigby's big bodyguard, Gus, looking for you, when you saw me there – oh yes, the people at Woolworths called the police right away when you escaped through the back door, so I knew you must have seen me. I had hoped I would be able to get the briefcase off you in Banbury, but you were quicker!"

"But weren't Rigby or his bodyguard suspicious when you knew exactly where we were all the time?"

"Well, you left plenty of clues behind you!"

"That was Alan's idea – his paper chase."

"Anyway, Rigby left me with Gus to work things out. He was not taking any chances. He flew to Scotland, where the gang's headquarters must be, and the other members of the gang are with him there now. It's near Fort William."

"But if you knew where we were, Rigby could have taken the briefcase off us at any time!"

"That wouldn't have been so easy, Heather. You always stayed together, and there were usually one or more witnesses. Attacking people in the busy streets of Glasgow was out of the question. We were hoping you would split up. Alan must have suspected this all the time. That's why he sent you on to Crianlarich with the briefcase."

"He didn't send me on," I protested. "He lost the key to his locker!"

"We were watching you both, Heather. As soon as you ran off to catch your train, Alan took the key out of his pocket and opened the locker. Gus and I thought he was sending you to safety, and that *he* had the money. Anyway, he put his backpack on and made one phone call – it must have been to the police – before he walked out of Queen Street Station straight into Gus's arms. We put Alan into the car, and I had to play my part as Rigby's accomplice. When

Gus found that Alan didn't have the briefcase, I had to think fast. Gus, the bodyguard, suggested that we should take Alan hostage and exchange him for the briefcase. Somehow I think this was what Alan wanted, too. Alan said you had gone on to Crianlarich, and I felt he had a reason for giving us this information, too. I telephoned Rigby to say that we knew where the money was, and that we had Alan as a hostage, but Rigby didn't trust an exchange of prisoner for money in the middle of a small village. It would be too risky. Someone might notice. He must have known that the police would not be far away. As we had his car, he said he would come down on the afternoon train to Crianlarich and see what was going on."

"I saw you when I got off the Fort William train," I said. "Did you see me?"

Cathy was surprised. "No, we were too busy discussing what to do with Alan. In the end Rigby and Gus drove back to their hideout with Alan. They left me here to contact you. They told me to bring you – and the money – to Rannoch Station on the morning train. They'll be waiting. They'll exchange Alan for the money."

"But is Alan safe? Suppose they think you are on our side?"

"Alan is quite safe. All Rigby wants is the money."

"But will you still be able to catch all the gang?"

"With some help from the police. Inspector March of Scotland Yard is coming later this evening. He has a plan ..."

"I hope it's better than Alan's," I said, as Mrs Macpherson called us in to dinner.

We had dinner more or less in silence, and very hungry I was by that time! Inspector March arrived, straight from London, and explained his plan. Cathy and I would take the early train to Rannoch Station. If the exchange was successful, the police would follow Rigby and, with luck, be able to arrest him and the rest of the gang. Help would not be far away if it were needed.

"Rigby's worried that we're getting very close to him," said Inspector March. "That's why he's chosen one of the loneliest places in Scotland for the exchange. We won't be able to get too close to him when he exchanges your brother for the briefcase, but there's only one road to the station. It runs east towards Kinloch Rannoch, and we'll have a car waiting there. We've been after this gang for almost six months and with the help of you two ladies we'll catch them all red-handed. May I see the briefcase now?"

I went up to my room and brought it downstairs.

The inspector counted the money carefully – to make sure we had not spent any of it, I suppose – and shut it again. The locks didn't seem to have suffered too badly from Alan's mistreatment on the train to Oxford. Inspector March checked the homing device. It was still working. With its help, the police would finally be able to round up the gang of forgers who had flooded the country with millions of pounds of forged banknotes.

"Aren't you going to replace the notes with newspaper or Monopoly money?" I asked.

He only laughed. "The first thing they'll do, Miss Taylor, is count the money. Then they'll let your brother go. If there's one banknote missing, they might get nasty. We can't take that risk. Whatever you do, do exactly as they say. They can't escape – unless they've got wings, of course!"

We all laughed.

"Well, that's about all we can do tonight. I'll see you at the station just before seven. I'd better take this briefcase with me. Good night."

But I didn't have a good night. It was midnight when the Inspector left, and I had to be up at six. Cathy slept well in the bed next to mine, but I tossed and turned all night. I was still worried about Alan, but there was nothing I could do. He had got himself – and me – into this mess, and we would have to get him out of it.

Chapter 13

We were at the station in good time for the train. Inspector March gave me the briefcase back, and Cathy and I boarded the train and sat in the coach just behind the sleeping cars from London.

I don't think I have ever been so nervous in my life. It was the kind of adventure which only happens once in a lifetime, so I tried to make the most of it. I've never known an hour pass so slowly, but finally the train began to slow down. This was it!

The train slid to a gentle stop and we got out, together with one or two backpackers who walked quickly off in the cool morning air through the grass and heather of the empty moorland around the station. The locomotive began to move slowly off towards Fort William. Cathy and I were left alone on the platform. There was no sign of the crooks or the big black car. Where were they? It was cool and windy on the open moor, and under my thin summer T-shirt I began to shiver.

Then I heard Alan's voice: "Heather! Over here!"

About three hundred metres away I could now see the figures of Alan and three or four men. One of them was Rigby. They had been hidden from the train behind a low hill. Gus was holding Alan firmly by the arm.

It was Rigby who spoke next: "Stay exactly where you are. We're coming over!" And he began walking towards us with one of the other men.

When they reached us, I handed over the briefcase without a word. Rigby watched us carefully while the other man opened the briefcase and quickly counted the money. "It's all there, boss," he said in an Australian accent.

"Well, you've kept your promise, so we'll keep ours." He waved towards the bodyguard, who released Alan's arm. Alan began walking towards us. "Goodbye, Cathy," said Rigby. "Thanks for your help. We're leaving the country now." He turned away and began to walk back to his men.

"Leaving the country? Now?" echoed Cathy. This was a completely new development. Inspector March had surely not expected this!.

"Aren't you taking me with you?" asked Cathy, taking one step forward. It sounded as if she really meant it. Rigby turned round again.

"Sorry, Cathy. We're leaving now, and there's no room for you on board."

"On board?" As she spoke we heard the sound of a helicopter starting up.

"Oh God!" whispered Cathy. "A helicopter! Why didn't we think of that! Inspector March was only making a joke when he said it, but they *have* got wings after all! With a helicopter, they can fly straight to Ireland! The British police can't touch them there!"

"What are we going to do?" I whispered.

"*Do*?" she hissed. "There's nothing we can do. They're going to escape!"

Then a miracle.

The other men had already boarded the helicopter, and Rigby had one foot on the step when the lid of the brief-case with the money suddenly sprang open. Alan must have broken part of the locking mechanism when he opened the case on the train to Oxford. The wind from the helicopter rotor immediately took control of the scattered banknotes and whirled them into the air in a mini snow-storm of coloured paper.

Rigby gave a loud shout and sprang off the step. Two other men jumped out. I could just about hear him say: "Stop the engine, you fool!" and the helicopter rotor slowed to a stop. Even the pilot jumped out to help.

The four crooks ran off wildly in all directions, chasing the fluttering banknotes, grabbing a £20 note here and a £50 note there. But it was hopeless. A high wind was now blowing, and most of the notes were fluttering across the open moor. Another kind of paper chase had begun.

Alan and I just stood there, helpless with laughter. Then we stopped laughing and watched, fascinated. The moor was suddenly alive with men in uniform. They sprang from their hiding places and quickly closed in from all sides. Inspector March had made his plans more carefully than we had made ours. Within minutes the first police car arrived from the direction of Kinloch Rannoch.

The members of the Rigby Gang were put into the waiting police cars, and that was the last we saw of them.

The search for the missing banknotes went on all day, but in the end the police only managed to find £95,955.

The other £4,045 is still out there somewhere, lying in the grass and heather of the lonely moor, moving from place to hiding place with every high wind that blows across this empty landscape. In a strange way, Alan's paper chase is still going on out there.

Vocabulary

Chapter 1

4	**to hitch-hike**	to travel by getting free rides in other people's cars or lorries

Chapter 2

5	**to pretend** [-'-]	to act as if s.th. were true
	Australian [ɒs'treɪljən]	
	briefcase	case used by businessmen for carrying documents
6	**bomb** [bɒm]	
	luggage	the cases and bags you have with you when you travel
	terrorist ['---]	
	to resist [-'-]	*widerstehen*
	sport *(Austral. slang)*	*here:* friend, pal, mate
	accent ['æksənt]	
	it's a deal	it's an agreement

Chapter 3

6	**description**	*Beschreibung*
	exit	the way out
7	**connection**	link
	suit	trousers and jacket worn by men
	spy	s.o. who has to find out secret information about another country
	buffet ['bʊfeɪ] **car**	part of a train where you can buy small snacks and drinks
	pale	without much colour

	to tear [teə], **tore, torn**	*zerreißen*
	forgery [ˈfɔ:dʒərɪ]	false copy

Chapter 4

8	**attendant**	assistant
	ultra-violet [ˈvaɪələt] **tester**	electronic machine that checks paper money
	banknote	piece of paper money
	consecutive [-ˈ---]	following one after the other
	to hand s.th. over to s.o.	to give s.th. to s.o.
	loot *(informal)*	stolen money or goods
	to realize	to know suddenly
	accomplice [əˈkʌmplɪs]	*Komplize*
	New Zealander [ˌnju:ˈzi:ləndə]	
9	**dud** *(informal)*	s.th. that does not work properly
	backpack	modern big rucksack
	to slide, slid, slid	*here:* to put in
	genuine [ˈdʒenjʊɪn]	real, true, not fake
	holy smoke!	*expression of surprise*
	to announce	to say s.th. officially, in public

Chapter 5

10	**terrified**	filled with fear
	inspector	*here:* person who checks tickets
	mate [meɪt] *(informal)*	friend, pal *(used by men)*
	how on earth ...?	*wie in aller Welt ...?*
	there is no need to do s.th.	there is no reason to do s.th.
	corridor	long narrow passage
	miserably *from* **miserable**	very unhappy
	fairly	quite
	whatever	*was auch immer*

	mysterious [mɪ'stɪərɪəs]	strange
	to wonder	to ask oneself
11	**in search** [sɜ:tʃ] **of**	looking for
	B+B	= bed and breakfast: cheap place for tourists to stay
	to solve	*lösen*
	mystery ['---]	s.th. strange that is hard to understand
	flood [ʌ]	*here:* a large number of s.th.
	inquiry	process of asking for information about s.th.
	to hiss	*zischen*
	to be involved in s.th.	to be taking part in s.th.
	to put into circulation [ˌsɜ:kjʊ:'leɪʃn]	to start to use

Chapter 6

12	**gently**	*here:* quietly
	in silence	without speaking
	item ['aɪtəm]	*here:* report
	to release [-'-]	*here:* to let go
	evidence	*Beweis*
	to wander	to walk around slowly
	Master Mind	TV quiz where difficult questions have to be answered
13	**to and fro**	backwards and forwards
	tongue [tʌŋ]	*Zunge*
	to wish	to want
	intelligent [ɪn'telɪdʒənt]	
	clerk [ɑ:]	person who works in an office, bank etc.

	suspiciously	*misstrauisch, argwöhnisch*
	to note	*here:* to write down
14	**I beg your pardon?**	sorry, what did you say?
	we'd better	it would be a good idea for us
	tenner *(informal)*	a ten-pound note
	nowadays	these days
	to go/do sightseeing	to visit a town or city and look at its famous buildings etc.
	it's a pity about s.th./s.o.	*es ist schade um etwas/jmd*
	unless	if not
	to give s.th. a miss	to decide not to do s.th.
	out of place	strange, not in the right place
15	**courtyard**	an open area between buildings
	heavyweight boxing champion	winner of boxing matches for boxers of the heaviest class

Chapter 7

16	**to put two and two together**	to work out the answer
	obviously	clearly
	idealist [aɪ'dɪəlɪst]	
	crusader	*here:* s.o. who works hard for s.th. he/she believes in
	to organize [ɔ:gənaɪz]	
	& Co.	= and Company (*here:* and gang)
	criminal	person who breaks the law
17	**crook** *(informal)*	criminal
	nasty	*here:* angry, unpleasant
	to double-cross *(informal)*	to cheat
	horrified	shocked
	to be on s.o.'s trail	to be following s.o.
	to be on the spot	to be right there

	to catch up with s.o.	to reach s.o.that one has been following
18	**to disappear**	*verschwinden*
	paper chase	*Schnitzeljagd*
	clue [klu:]	s.th. that gives information about a problem
	suitable	of the right kind
	to shiver	to shake with fear or cold

Chapter 8

18	**to cheer s.o. up**	to make s.o. happy
19	**on our track**	on our trail
	heading for	on the way to
	plenty of	a lot of
	cab	*here:* front part of a lorry where the driver sits
	och [ɒx] (*Scottish)*	oh
	ye [ji:] **(***Scottish)*	you
	Scots	Scottish
	bonnie (*Scottish)*	beautiful, pretty
	scenery ['si:nərɪ]	landscape
	grand	wonderful, very beautiful
	motorway (*GB*)	*Autobahn*
20	**rather**	*here: lieber*
	moorland	high area of open ground
	to be surrounded by s.th.	to have s.th. around it
	to drop s.o.	to let s.o. out of a car
	depot ['depəʊ]	place where lorries, buses etc are kept when not being used
21	**headline**	title of a newspaper article

	glamour girl	famous beautiful woman
	to vanish	to disappear
	well-built	(of a man) big and strong
	Ms [mɪz]	modern for *Miss* or *Mrs* when one does not want to say if a woman is married or not
	spokesman	person who speaks for a group
	to suspect [-'-]	*here:* to think that s.th. is true
	foul [aʊ] **play**	(crime which leads to) murder
22	**to kidnap** ['--]	to "steal" a person
	to mention	to talk about
	hint	indirect suggestion, clue

Chapter 9

23	**to check out**	to leave a hotel after paying
	accommodation	room, place to stay in
	in advance	*im voraus*
	premonition [ˌpriːmə'nɪʃn]	a feeling that s.th. (unpleasant) is going to happen
24	**locker**	cupboard for storing luggage at railway stations etc. that can be locked
	somehow	in some way
	bait [beɪt]	food used to catch fish or animals
25	**actually**	really, in fact
	to take a risk	to do s.th. dangerous
	to switch	to (ex)change
26	**sticky**	*here:* hot and uncomfortable
	sergeant ['sɑːdʒənt]	police officer (second rank)
	to leave (our) options open	not to decide what to do

27	**due** [dju:] **to do s.th.**	supposed to/expected to do s.th.
	disaster [-'--]	s.th. terrible that happens
	precious ['preʃəs]	*here:* very important
	to tick away	(of time) to pass
	damn and blast it *(vulgar)*	*expression showing anger*
	left-luggage office	place in stations where people can leave their luggage for a time
	to panic	to become very frightened
	to split up, split, split	to break up, to separate
	to board	*here:* to get on

Chapter 10

28	**to dodge** [dɒdʒ]	to move away quickly
29	**to echo** ['ekəʊ]	*widerhallen*
	to signal ['--]	to give a clear sign
	an age	a very long time
	in the distance	far away
	to approach	to come nearer
	to come in sight	to come close enough to be seen
	to recognize s.o.	to know who s.o. is

Chapter 11

30	**to reach out**	to put out a hand
	terraced house	house joined to others in a row
	contribution [ˌkɒntrɪ'bju:ʃn]	*Beitrag*
31	**ecological** [ˌi:kə'lɒdʒɪkl]	
	wherever	*wo auch immer*
	lips	*Lippen*

Chapter 12

31	**to protest** [-'-]	
	cheek	*Wange*
32	**inspector**	*here:* police officer of higher rank than a sergeant
	official [ə'fɪʃl]	
	Security Branch	*Sicherheitsabteilung*
	to replace	to put s.th. in place of another
	excellent ['eksələnt]	very good
33	**homing device**	a little electronic machine that gives signals so that its position can be found
	to distinguish	to tell apart
34	**headquarters** [ˌ-'--]	main meeting place of an organization
	witness	a person who sees s.o. doing s.th.
35	**hostage** ['hɒstɪdʒ]	*Geisel*
	hideout	a place where s.o. can hide
36	**to be successful**	*here:* to work out as planned
	to catch s.o. red-handed	to catch s.o. when he/she is in the middle of doing s.th.
	to suffer	*here:* to be damaged
	mistreatment	bad way of treating s.th.
	to round up	*here:* to catch all together
	wing	*Flügel*
37	**to toss and turn**	to move from side to side (in bed)

Chapter 13

37	**coach**	*here:* part of a train
	heather ['heðə]	*Heide(kraut)*
38	**miracle** ['mɪrəkl]	s.th. wonderful and surprising
39	**mechanism** ['mekənɪzm]	
	rotor ['rəʊtə]	the wings on top of the helicopter
	to whirl [wɜ:l]	to move round quickly
	to flutter	to fly with small, quick movements
	to be alive with	to be full of